6/08

The Book of
HAPPY THINGS

SO-BTZ-527

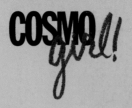

The Book of
HAPPY THINGS

The Editors of CosmoGirl!

HEARST BOOKS
A division of Sterling Publishing Co., Inc.

New York / London
www.sterlingpublishing.com

Close your eyes and think of the things that make you happy. There are tons of them, right? Whether it's a major event (scoring the game-winning goal! Your first kiss!) or just the simpler stuff (hanging out with your friends or watching a sunset), life's full of happy moments. And because we love to see you flashing those pearly whites, we asked you to send in your most favorite things in the whole entire world. You know, stuff that makes you break out into a goofy grin just *thinking* about them.

So whenever you're in need of a boost, or you just want to feel all warm and fuzzy inside, simply turn to any page in this book. Then, sit back, relax, and be happy, CG!

XO,

Susan

Susan Schulz
Editor in Chief, CosmoGIRL!

Eating

Taking a nice,

LONG MIDDAY NAP

and waking up

feeling energized and

ready for anything!

waffles for dinner!

Making a
PHOTO COLLAGE
of all of your pics,
and thinking about
how much you
love your friends
every time you look at it!

Staying up all night
with your friends
reliving every moment
of your

SWEET SIXTEEN.

Eating a huge
ICE CREAM CONE
as it drips down your arm
on a hot, hot day—
and fighting off the
**inevitable ice cream
headache!**

A hot pair of
sunglasses
that make you
FEEL LIKE A STAR
every time you slip them on.

The view from
the top of a really
TALL BUILDING.

GIVING OUT CANDY

to cute little kids

on Halloween night.

Lighting **sparklers**

THAT ONE INSIDE JOKE

you have with
your friends that always
makes you break into
uncontrollable
giggle fits!

on the fourth of July.

Taking
GOOFY PICTURES
with your friends,
then posting them online
and leaving
hilarious comments
for each other.

The moment you pull on
A PAIR OF JEANS
and think,
*"These make me
look amazing!"*

When your
mom comes through
and buys you that
EXTRA-SPECIAL GIFT
you've been
hinting about forever.

Hearing your parents
tell the story about the

DAY YOU WERE BORN

every year
on your birthday!

Getting a **huge hug**

that lifts you

That moment
when you find out
YOUR MAJOR CRUSH
is interested in you too.

Reading messages
from friends
in old yearbooks and journals
and reliving all of those great
FORGOTTEN MOMENTS.

off the ground.

Going out of your way
to do something
FOR A FRIEND
just because you love her.

DONATING
part of your
part-time job's paycheck
to your favorite charity.

Waking up to find
your cat
CUDDLING
with you on your bed.

Layering on a
**FUZZY SWEATER,
MITTENS, AND SCARF**
on the first chilly day
of the year.

The day you
finally get your
BRACES OFF!

Leaving the
dentist with
NO CAVITIES!

Getting
prom dress inspiration
as you watch your
FAVORITE CELEBRITIES
walk the red carpet
at an awards show.

Wearing your

FAVORITE FLIRTY DRESS

to a casual occasion,

just to spice things up.

Going for a bike ride on
A BEAUTIFUL DAY
and feeling like you can
go on forever.

Playing the sport you love,
like field hockey or soccer,
and looking up at the
scoreboard to see that
YOU'RE WINNING
10-zip!

Watching the **sunset** fron

Realizing that your **LITTLE SIBLINGS** **are pretty cool kids—** even though they do get into your stuff once in a while!

an empty beach at dusk.

The comfy

FRESHNESS

of new underwear
and socks.

Knowing that
no matter how worn out
YOUR FAVORITE
old sweats are,
you'll never
get rid of them!

Hearing your parents say

"We're *so*

LAUGHING

so hard with your

friends

that you get an

abs workout!

proud of you."

SHARING EVERYTHING—
from clothes to your
toothbrush (*sometimes!*)—
with your best friend.

Watching old
HOME VIDEOS,
especially those priceless
moments like your
10th birthday when you
were so excited to get
your very first cell phone!

THAT MOMENT

you finally

GET OVER

the guy who
broke your heart,
and realize that *he's*
the one missing out.

Reading an

AMAZING HOROSCOPE

that makes you

excited about

your day.

Scooping up a
golden retriever puppy
in your arms and getting
covered with
SLOBBERY KISSES!

Swinging

ON A SWING

and feeling like you're

six years old again.

Taking a road trip
WITH YOUR FAMILY
and to your surprise,
actually having fun!

Catching a wave in the

ocean and riding

The whoosh of air that fills your ears **as you ski down** a huge mountain.

it all the way in!

Getting asked out
by the guy you've been
LUSTING AFTER
from the moment
you laid eyes on him!

WHEN A CUTE GUY
flashes you a shy smile
as he passes you
in the hallway.

The first

kiss with your crush!

Walking out of a

exam

FINDING TEN BUCKS

in the pocket of
a pair of jeans
or a coat you haven't
worn in a while.

knowing you aced it.

Opening up
your mailbox and
seeing a big, fat
acceptance letter.

Having your

WHOLE FAMILY

there to

watch you graduate.

Jumping up and

DANCING

the instant you hear

your new

favorite song!

THAT GIDDY FEELING

your get when your

plane's about to land

and you're going

somewhere

super exciting.

The sound of a

SKATEBOARD CRUISING

down the sidewalk.
*(Which usually means a hot
guy is coming your way!)*

SEEING FRIENDS

for the first time
after a long break
from school.

COMFORT FOODS
like grilled cheese
and tomato soup
or homemade
mac-n-cheese!

Anything with

**PEANUT BUTTER
AND CHOCOLATE!**

Walking into

YOUR KITCHEN

and being greeted
by the smell of your

favorite meal

cooking.

Looking up at a
STAR-FILLED SKY
and searching
for constellations.

Getting up at 2 a.m.
to watch a
**METEOR SHOWER
OR ECLIPSE.**

Snuggling close
with someone
as you watch
LIGHTNING BOLTS
zig-zagging
across the sky
during a raging storm.

SNORKELING

in crystal-clear waters

surrounded by a

school of tropical fish

in the most amazing colors.

SUNNY DAYS

when the weatherman

said it would rain.

When a **cute boy**

Looking like a

REAL-LIFE PRINCESS

in your dream dress and

sparkly tiara

on prom night.

That moment you
slip on your

DREAM PROM DRESS

and say to yourself,

"This is the one."

holds a door open for you.

RAIDING YOUR FRIDGE
then plopping down
on the couch
to watch *General Hospital*
after school.

Indulging in an extra
topping—or two!—

The

mouthwatering smell

that fills your nose

when you open up a box of

DELIVERY PIZZA.

on your frozen yogurt.

Watching a horror movie

WHILE CUDDLING

on the couch

with your sweetie—

especially when you make
him tell you what's happening
as you're covering your eyes
during the scariest parts!

When you finish a
conversation with someone
and realize you've been
smiling the entire time.

Getting a

real letter from a **friend**

A BRAND-NEW JOURNAL

thick with blank pages
just begging for you to fill up
with all of your thoughts,
hopes, and dreams.

who's moved far away.

THAT FEELING

when you just start liking

someone, but don't want

to admit it—

even though it's

probably obvious

because you get giddy

every time he walks by!

THAT FIRST WARM DAY
of the year when
you can get away
with wearing shorts
and flip-flops.

Going out for

Frappuccinos with

Meeting
SOMEONE NEW
and having the distinct
feeling that she's going
to be a great friend.

Blasting *anything* by
Justin Timberlake
while getting ready
to go out on a
SATURDAY NIGHT.

your besties!

Showing off your double-jointed thumbs or busting out your robot dance just to get **A FEW LAUGHS** from your friends.

Making up **SILLY DANCE ROUTINES to 80's songs** and performing them for anyone who'll watch!

Hitting up a

YARD SALE

and discovering a

fabulous

FAUX FUR JACKET.

Sweet!

FINDING SOMETHING

that you thought

you'd lost forever.

Embellishing your jeans
with funky patches,
then feeling

proud

that you

CREATED SOMETHING

so cool with your
own two hands!

Tripping in front of
everyone in a crowded
hallway—and being able to
LAUGH IT OFF!

Walking out of school on a
Friday afternoon with the
WHOLE WEEKEND
ahead of you.

Scraping up every last bit
of a bowlful of
VANILLA ICE CREAM
topped with
hot fudge and caramel.

Licking
FLUFFY PINK FROSTING
off your lips as you eat
a huge cupcake.

Watching your

BABY COUSIN

sleep.

Landing your

DREAM INTERNSHIP.

Even better?

When it pays, too!

GREAT ADVICE

from someone you really

respect and admire.

Celebrating big moment

at a **fancy** restauran

with a delicious meal

Having to catch your breath **every time**

CHECKING OUT HOTTIES

at the beach from behind
your dark sunglasses
so they don't know you're
looking their way!

you pass by your **crush**.

Not having to
set an alarm, and
JUST SLEEPING IN
'til whenever you want!

SNUGGLING
under lots of thick,
warm blankets
on a cold night.

Raiding your **SUPER-GLAM** friend's closet to find **a cool outfit** to wear to the school dance.

Enjoying **SOMETHING CULTURAL,** like a new museum exhibit, the ballet, or anything that would make **your parents proud.**

Being home alone and
**SINGING AT THE TOP
OF YOUR LUNGS**
and dancing like crazy just
because no one's around.

Collecting
QUIRKY THINGS,
like rubber ducks
or old-fashioned buttons.

Feeling your

CAT'S PURRS

throughout your body

as she falls asleep

in your lap.

Smelling that

FAMILIAR SCENT

of your house after you've

been away for a while.

Flipping over your **pillow**

and feeling the cold side.

Settling in for that
new movie
you've been waiting
months to see with a
big bucket of
BUTTERED POPCORN
on your lap.

Getting in a

good ol' cry

while watching a

TEARJERKER MOVIE.

Watching

DISNEY MOVIES

and singing along

to all of the songs

with your friends

who aren't embarrassed

to admit they know

the words, too!

Slumber parties!

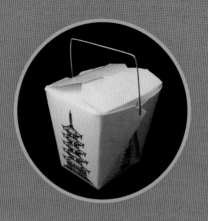

ENJOYING RITUALS

with your family
like Chinese take-out
on Fridays or
movie nights on Sundays.

Realizing that it's **not the end of the world** if you don't have **A BOYFRIEND.**

That moment when
**YOU FIRST HOLD HANDS
with your boyfriend—**
your palm is so sweaty,
but you don't want to
pull your hand away!

When your boyfriend
BRINGS YOU FLOWERS—
even if he bought them
at the gas station!

Cracking open a

NEW BOX OF

CRAYONS

and going to town
in a coloring book—
just like you

used to do as a kid!

Ordering a
KIDS' MEAL
at a fast food restaurant
just to get the toy!

DRAWING
faces and flowers
with your fingers on
**fogged-up
car windows.**

When your boyfriend
pulls away from a kiss
just to look
INTO YOUR EYES.

Cute guys who actually
take the time to have a
GENUINE CONVERSATION
with you.

Stepping outside
on a gorgeous
SPRING MORNING
with the birds chirping
as though they're singing
just for you.

Rolling down a
huge, grassy hill or
SPINNING AROUND
in circles
until you're too dizzy
to stand up.

Spending an afternoon making **SANDCASTLES** at the beach.

Dipping your
FRESHLY-PAINTED TOES
into the pool for the first
time each summer.

Spa treatments,
like at-home
MANI/PEDIS,
that make you feel
totally relaxed
and pampered.

Making yourself over
with a new eyeliner
and mascara and feeling
LIKE A SUPERMODEL
afterwards!

Getting up the courage to
try something
TOTALLY DIFFERENT,
like chopping off
your long locks
for a chic, short 'do.

TOSSING OUT
your notebook
after your final exam on
the last day of class.

Being singled out
for doing
something really well,
like when your
English teacher reads
your story aloud
to the entire class.

Spending a
warm summer night
FLOATING
on an inner tube
in your backyard pool.

New friend request

That awesome

STRESS-FREE FEELING

where you've got
nothing to worry about.

SINGING

at the top of your lungs to
"Don't Stop Believing"
with your teammates on
the way to a big
volleyball tournament.

or messages on your wall.

Being

SUPER PRODUCTIVE

and getting all of your work
for the entire week
done in one night!

Having **absolutel**

nothing to do.

Hearing such
GREAT NEWS—
making the cheerleading
squad or snagging the lead
in the school play—that you
can't wait to share it
with everyone you see.

SINGING IN THE CAR
with your friends,
with the radio turned up
and the windows rolled down.

Getting absorbed in
A GOOD BOOK—
one of those page-turners
you can't even think
about putting down
until you've devoured
every word.

Long, quiet walks tho

let you think and

Having your own little

CORNER OF THE WORLD—

a tree house,

a clearing in a field—

where you can go

and just get lost

in your thoughts.

:lear your head.

Those blissful,
love-filled days of a
NEW RELATIONSHIP
when just the thought
of your boyfriend
makes you break out into
a huge smile!

Apple picking

in the fall.

Discovering
you have a
NEW TALENT.

When a guy
COMPLIMENTS YOU
on something,
like your new shirt or
the color of your eyes.

SUMMER NIGHTS
that are just
chilly enough for a hoodie
or long-sleeved tee.

Kissing for hours

and hours!

Trying out

NEW FOODS.

(Who knew

sushi

could actually be delish?).

Hitting a café with
your friends and getting into
GREAT DISCUSSIONS
over caramel macchiatos.

Running into an old friend
and realizing
TRUE FRIENDSHIPS
never end.

A school night with
NO HOMEWORK!

How
SOFT AND SMOOTH
your legs feel
after you shave them.

Solving a
SUDOKU PUZZLE
faster than your
brainiac sister!

The look on your
brother's face
when you
BEAT HIM
at Wii Tennis (*again!*).

Knowing that even when
you do something dumb,
YOUR PARENTS ARE STILL
GOING TO LOVE YOU
no matter what.

That first
BIG HUG
from your dad when he
greets you at the airport
after a long trip.

That huge
FEELING OF RELIEF
when you write
the last line of a
15-page history paper.

Getting a random
text message or e-mail from
AN OLD FRIEND
that you haven't heard from
in a long time.

Spending the

FIRST BIG SNOW DAY

outside sledding and
having huge snow ball fights.
Then coming inside
for hot chocolate—
with mini marshmallows!

Making **footprints** in

freshly-fallen snow.

BRINGING SOUVENIRS
back for your friends after
you've traveled somewhere
faraway and exotic.

Striking up a
CONVERSATION
with the person sitting
next to you on a plane.

CHILLAXING

in a warm

vanilla-scented

bubble bath

after a stressful day

WARM TOWELS

fresh out of

the dryer.

Buying yourself
FRESH FLOWERS
to place by your bed
so you have something
pretty to wake up to.

and watching them

That first **BURST OF FLAVOR** as you bite into a big piece **of fruity-flavored gum.**

Blowing bubbles outside blow away.

Jumping into a pool
**WITH YOUR
CLOTHES ON!**

Three-day
WEEKENDS!

Making

new friends!

DAYDREAMING

about your future.

FALLING ASLEEP

in a hammock as the
warm breeze gently
tickles you.

A DREAM

so good

that when you wake up,

you try to force yourself

back to sleep

so you can pick up

where you left off!

Getting

NEW BLING

from your parents on

your 15th birthday.

Feeling the ocean
rush over your feet
as you take a romantic
BEACH STROLL
in the sand with
your sweetie.

Finally getting
the nerve up
to ask out your crush—
AND HE SAYS YES!

Laying on the grass
and searching for different
SHAPES IN THE CLOUDS.

Seeing something
UNEXPECTED IN THE SKY,
like a blimp, a hot air balloon,
or an eagle.

JUMPING

in puddles when

you're wearing

cute rain boots!

Walking outside

after a rainstorm

and suddenly spotting

A RAINBOW IN THE SKY.

Planting a **garden** in your backyard

Sticking your nose into a

HONEYSUCKLE BUSH

growing in your backyard

and breathing in the

sweet scent.

and watching it grow.

Overhearing
someone say
SOMETHING NICE
about you.

Dotting your
i's with hearts
or smiley faces,
JUST BECAUSE
you feel like it!

SHAKING

what your mama

gave you

when the DJ plays

Fergalicious at a party.

Trading
ESKIMO KISSES
with the 4-year-old
you baby-sit for.

TEACHING
a kindergartener
how to tie his shoes.

Spending a
rainy day playing
OLD-SCHOOL GAMES,
like Candy Land or Twister
with the little girl who
lives next door.

TAKING WALKS
with your best friend,
talking about everything.

Friday night
AT THE DINER
with friends after
a long week.

Celebrating

YOUR BIRTHDAY

somewhere different
and exciting, like
on the beach.

Painting

A MURAL

on your

bedroom wall.

Giving your

ROOM A FACELIFT

by repainting the walls in

your favorite color

and replacing your

kiddie furniture with

funky stuff you found

at a thrift store.

BIRTHDAY CELEBRATIONS

with tons of presents, cake,
friends, and a tiara for the
birthday girl!

Window shopping at

expensive boutiques.

Riding the new

ROLLER COASTER

at an amusement park and

screaming your head off

during the entire ride!

Shooting down a

TWISTY WATERSLIDE!

When a friend

DROPS EVERYTHING

just to be with you when

you really need her.

Treating a friend to a

MILKSHAKE

when she's had a bad day.

When your
mom brings you
chicken noodle soup,
and a ton of
CELEBRITY MAGS
when you're stuck in bed
with the flu.

Hearing your phone ring,
looking at the ID,
and realizing
IT'S *THE* CALL
you've been waiting for.

Hearing the first song
you slow danced to
WITH YOUR CRUSH
and smiling as you
relive the moment.

Being told you're

a good kisser.

EARLY FALL DAYS

when the air's a bit crisper
and the leaves crunch
beneath your feet.

Homemade
APPLE PIE.

Drinking hot chocolate
on a rainy day while
SNUGGLING UP
with your boyfriend
and watching VH1!

Gulping soda so fast
that the

Getting out all of your
bottled-up frustrations
with a loud,

CRAZY SCREAM!

bubbles make you tear up!

Lounging
ON THE BEACH
with your friends
and trading gossip mags.

Sitting in class during
the last days of school
before summer break and
DAYDREAMING
of the beach, the pool,
and picnics in the park.

REWARDING YOURSELF

on your way home with a
strawberry smoothie after
working your butt off
at track practice.

Giving a friend a
SUPER-THOUGHTFUL GIFT
for her birthday,
like notecards
personalized with her name.

Hearing your boyfriend

finally mumble

That moment
when you find out
YOUR MAJOR CRUSH
is interested in you too.

I love you for the first time.

Programming
A HOT GUY'S NUMBER
in your cell phone.

STORING PICS
of friends on your phone
and scrolling through them
when you're bored.

Planning your next
GREAT ADVENTURE,
like backpacking
through Europe
with your best friend.

Going to airports and
WATCHING PLANES
take off and land.

Those amazingly
ROMANTIC MOMENTS
when it feels like you
and your guy are the
only two people
in the world.

Seeing an elderly couple
WALKING TOGETHER,
arm-in-arm, and realizing
that true love really *can*
last forever.

for the first time

Getting your

DRIVER'S LICENSE!

Getting a

PARKING SPOT

near the mall

on the busiest

shopping day of the year.

Driving down the highway

on your own.

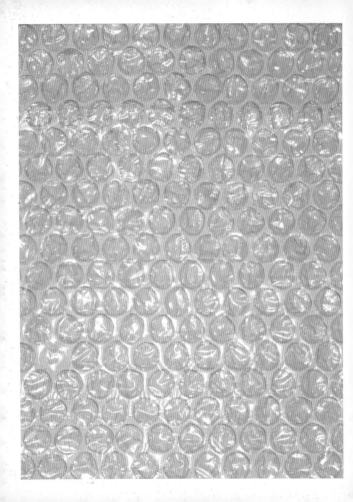

Getting a big package
in the mail and then
popping all of the
BUBBLE WRAP
that comes with it!

Holiday dinners

Making a favorite
FAMILY RECIPE
on your own
for the very first time.

Realizing your parents
are cooler
than you
originally thought.

with the fam!

Making

HOMEMADE SMOOTHIES

with the berries you

hand-picked

with your friends.

Showing off your

LEGS IN HIGH HEELS—

especially after you've
been working out!

VINTAGE JEWELRY

that looks like a
million dollars,
even if it cost you only
three bucks.

Correctly answering
questions on
QUIZ SHOWS
and realizing
how much stuff
you've got stored
in your brain.

When you finally
come up with a
SOLUTION
for that one
huge problem
that's been
bugging you.

The way your dog
looks at you like
YOU'RE THE ONLY ONE
in his world.

How excited your dog gets
when you say the words
"WALK" AND "TREAT"!

Biting into a

Grabbing two spoons—and **YOUR LITTLE SISTER—** and sitting down to eat **rocky road ice cream** right out of the carton and getting her **to gossip about** all of the cute guys at her school.

juicy peach

Answering the phone
on your birthday and
hearing your family singing,
"HAPPY BIRTHDAY"
on the other end.

Scoring tickets to your favorite band's concert and going

ABSOLUTELY NUTS

as they play all of their best songs.

GOING OUT

for burgers and fries with **your whole crew.**

Long kisses i

Lighting up

at the sight of

YOUR BOYFRIEND'S FACE

after being apart

for a while.

the rain!

A warm,

FUDGY BROWNIE

and a cold glass of milk
to wash it down.

Picking up

CUPCAKES

from an adorable bakery,
then sharing them
with friends.

Spending a

SUNDAY NIGHT

watching a football game

with your

dad and brothers.

Long, steaming hot

showers—especially

Noticing

NEW MUSCLES

on your body after just a few

weeks of working out.

Ice cold

BOTTLES OF WATER

on a boiling hot day.

after a hard workout.

Watching your friend

count go up

GOING ONLINE
and seeing that the
cute guy you met
last summer at the beach just
signed on, too.

Talking to your friends
**ONLINE 'TIL ONE
IN THE MORNING,**
even though you know
you'll see them the next day.

on **Facebook.**

SINGING IN THE SHOWER,

pretending like

you're trying out

for the next season of

American Idol.

Hearing a song
that speaks to you
so directly,
it's as though it was
WRITTEN JUST FOR YOU.

The sound of your
DOG'S SNORES
when he's in a
super deep sleep.

Going to the zoo
and seeing
adorable
BABY ANIMALS!

Baking—and eating!—
**chocolate chip
cookies**
from scratch.

Anything in a

HAWAIIAN PRINT.

Even better when it's

worn in the winter!

Waking up
in the morning with a
SMILE ON YOUR FACE
as you look forward to
what you're going to be
doing that day.

Waking up
and realizing you
still have a few hours
left to sleep.

Finding out
YOU WON A CONTEST
you entered so long ago,
you'd forgotten
all about it.

Getting a
HOLE-IN-ONE
when you're playing
mini golf.

Jumping

on a trampoline!

Speaking a

SECOND LANGUAGE

well enough to use it
outside of the classroom.

Landing an

AWESOME SUMMER JOB

that's so much fun,
it doesn't even
feel like work!

WORKING REALLY HARD
at something,
like a sport or a
super-tough subject
in school—
and seeing yourself
GETTING BETTER
every time you go at it.

FINALLY FINISHING

a huge

end-of-the-year project

that you thought

you'd never get through.

The sound of the

SCHOOL BELL

at the end of the day.

When your guy tells you that
YOU'RE BEAUTIFUL
even when your face
is swollen from getting your
wisdom teeth pulled!

CHATTING
with your boyfriend
late at night, then
falling asleep smiling.

Shy,

sweet guys.

Listening to your mom
tell stories about the
SILLY THINGS
you used to say or do
as a kid!

GETTING A GIFT CARD

for your favorite store,

then going on a

guilt-free shopping spree

with it!

Finding that one shirt

you've been lusting after

on the

SALE RACK—

in your size!

Getting a

HUGE CHUNK

of cookie in your

cookies and cream

ice cream!

Whipping up a

VANILLA MILKSHAKE

that's so thick,

you have to eat it

with a spoon!

MAKING FRIENDS

with someone
completely different
from you.

Landing a seat next to
THE NEW, HOT GUY
in your algebra class
on the first day of school.
(Hooray for assigned seating!)

Seeing your guy's
JAW DROP
when you show up
to a party
wearing a hot dress.

Waking up on
SUNDAY MORNING
and having a big,
yummy breakfast
with your family.

VEGGING OUT
and watching
old episodes of
Friends.

Realizing all of a sudden
while you're out with friends
that it's one of those days
you'll remember
FOREVER.

Spending an entire day
**talking in
FUNNY ACCENTS.**

When you take a

SCHOOL PICTURE

that you're

really happy with!

Opening up your

NEW YEARBOOK

for the first time
and turning right to an

awesome picture

of you and your friends.

MAKING S'MORES

in the microwave
on a rainy day.

CAMPING OUT
in your best friend's
backyard,
roasting marshmallows
and sleeping
under the stars!

When your
hair falls
JUST THE WAY
you want it to.

Having someone
PLAY WITH YOUR HAIR.

Swimming until

Running into the

COOL OCEAN

on a steamy day
the *second* you hit the beach.

you're **pruned!**

'

So, what makes *you*

HAPPY?

Have your own list of
happy things? Grab a pen
and use this space to
write down whatever
makes you smile.

When your
new issue of

arrives in the mail!